Easy words to read
Big pig on a dig

Phil Roxbee Cox
Illustrated by Stephen Cartwright
Edited by Jenny Tyler

Language consultant:
Marlynne Grant
BSc, CertEd, MEdPsych, PhD, AFBPs, CPsychol

There is a little yellow duck to find on every page.

First published in 1999 by Usborne Publishing Ltd. Usborne House, 83-85 Saffron Hill, London EC1N 8RT, England. www.usborne.com
Copyright © 1999 Usborne Publishing Ltd.

Big Pig gets a letter.

Look for
this hat.

Big Pig

Big Pig sees the hat.

There is a map in the hat.

Big Pig runs
to Fat Cat.

4

"Where to dig?
Dig for what,
Big Pig?"

"Gold!" grunts Big Pig.
"Old gold."

6

"Fat Cat! Look at the map in this hat."

dig

"It shows where to dig, Fat Cat."

Map

"But I am a cat.
Cats need to nap.
I am a napping cat."

"You dig, Big Pig.
Be a pig on a dig."

"Let me nap

and dream of cream."

Big Pig sees three green trees.

Big Pig sees three green trees on the map.

Big Pig is happy.

He pops on a wig.

Big Pig is happy.

He hops on a twig. He can go on a dig!

"I am a happy big pig on a dig."

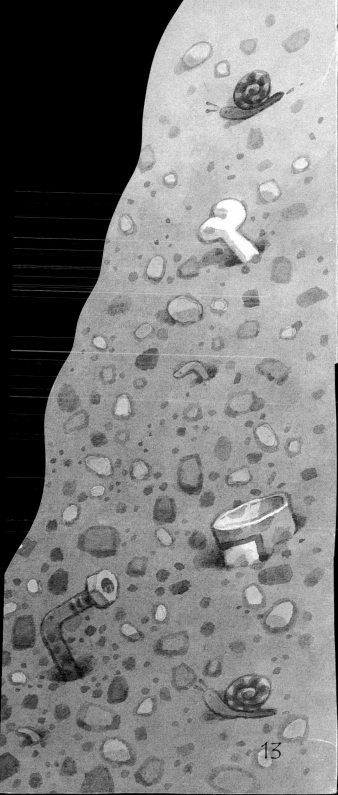

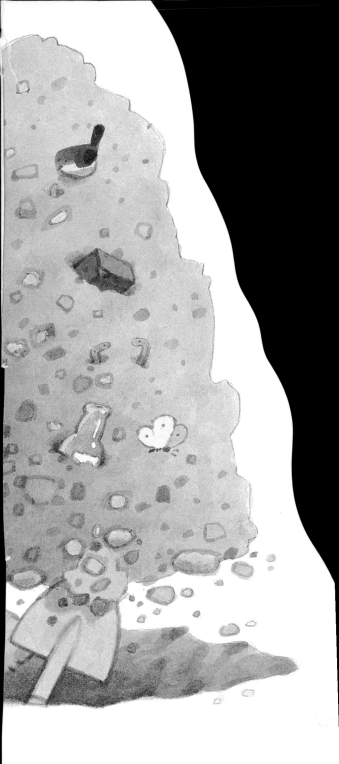

"I dig down

and down

and... down."

What has Big Pig found...

...down in the ground?

Fat Cat grins.

"I drew the
map for fun,"
he says.

It's Funny Bunny.

"There's no
old gold here."

Big Pig grins. "Digging is fun too!"